AMISH SPRING

Amish Sisterhood

Tara Price

Published by Trellis Publishing, 2021.

AMISH SISTERHOOD

First edition. June 26, 2021.

Copyright © 2021 Tara Price.

ISBN: 979-8224844623

Written by Tara Price.

Katie sighed as she watched her younger sister, Mary, rapped her fingers on the nightstand. In her other hand, she held her worn bible.

"Mary, please don't tap your nails on the nightstand."

"Sorry, Katie." The young girl sighed, and held the bible in both hands now. She lowered it to look at her sister. "I'm bored."

"I know it's tough to be bedridden. As soon as your leg heals, you'll be able to walk again." The community doctor had told her that as soon as her leg had healed, and she could walk on her own, Mary would be able to take off and go on her *rumspringa*. She had been looking forward to it for a year; she wanted more education.

The entire community was sure that Mary would be the one who got lost before baptism. Katie had returned from hers the week before Mary's leg was broken in a freak horse-riding accident. She had found many of the boys creepy and had almost been killed once because she was in what the locals deemed a 'bad part' of town.

At any rate, she had cut hers short by two weeks and returned home. She was to be baptized the next day, but with Mary's leg, she had postponed her baptism.

"Willis comes home today." Mary spoke up again. "You know, Mark's Willis." Katie looked up. "I hear he missed you."

"Shush, Mary. You're supposed to be reading."

"You know I can't read in bed." Her sister sighed deeply. "If you're so worried, read to me." Katie picked up her own bible as her sister continued to complain. "Hey. I'm in Leviticus."

"Alright." She managed a smile. However, as she read her sister Leviticus 2 aloud, she wasn't sure how she felt. Willis M. Wittmer had always been a bit of a rowdy boy. No one had expected him to return after his *rumspringa*, but she had always felt there was something different about him. His brown hair grew too fast for his mother to keep up with it, and so he would sometimes get away with wearing his hair longer than he should have.

Either way, everyone had been incredibly excited that he was coming home. He would be getting baptized within the week, and if Mary felt she could get on without her for about an hour, she would go. She hadn't realized she had stopped reading aloud.

"Katie?" Mary's voice interrupted her thoughts. "Katie?"

"Huh?" She looked up from the pages of the bible. "What?" Her sister laughed a little, and she looked down at the bible again. It fell off her lap, and onto the floor.

"You're daydreaming, again, aren't you?" She smiled widely. "You're thinking about *Willis*. Aren't you?"

"Am I that easy to read?" She shifted uncomfortably in her chair.

"Honey, if only I could find love that easily."

"I'm not in love." She felt her cheeks becoming even hotter than they usually were. The words came out in a mutter, and she could feel her sister's eyes on her. She didn't dare to look up again.

"Katie! You have a visitor." Their mother's voice floated up the house.

"I'll be back as soon as possible, Mary." She picked the bible up off the floor before setting it on the table. Then, she walked down to the living room as quickly as possible.

"Hello, Katie." A masculine voice echoed in her ears. Her eyes fell on a buff 18 year old with familiar blue eyes.

"Willis..." She smiled a little. "How have you been?"

"Anxious to come home." He returned her smile. "And you?"

"I've had my fair share of homesickness too." She stayed on the far side of the room. "I hear you're to be baptized soon. Congratulations."

"Thank you. Have I heard correctly that you're getting baptized soon as well?" He took a couple steps closer, but still had a lot of room to cover.

"Yes." She smiled a little wider.

"Congratulations, Katie." His smile widened as well. "I should probably get going. Is Mary still bedridden?"

"Unfortunately. How did you hear?"

"My mother told me shortly after I arrived home. She told me not to bother you much today." She couldn't help but laugh a little bit.

"Thanks. I'll see you around?" He laughed a little now, nodded, and began to walk out the door. She didn't try to stop him. However, she did notice that he had changed.

Instead of being excited about being out in the world, he had said that he was anxious to come home. Anxious to come home meant that he missed something about their lifestyle. He missed something, or someone, bad enough to forgo everything he had thought he wanted after his *rumspringa*. Not only that, but he had bulked up while he was away. Even with daily work on the farm, the men in her community weren't too muscular or strong. More often, they had the bare minimum so that they could do their job without being sore all day, every day.

He'd also grown taller. Willis had been slightly taller than her when she left; now he was about a foot taller. His smile had become a little more radiant, and he was no longer itching to get away from their lifestyle.

Katie returned upstairs slowly, thinking over his words and turning them around and around in her head. In her long blue dress, she certainly had no attractive features to show off except for the light dusting of freckles across her cheek and nose, and her light brown eyes. Her parents often said that if her commitment to their lifestyle didn't attract the boys, her eyes would.

"Who was it, Katie?" Mary tried to sit up, but groaned.

"Easy, sister." She helped her lie down again. "It was Willis."

"Mark's Willis?"

"The same." She smiled a little. "He's home, and getting baptized, as you said he was going to do."

"You should trust me more often, shouldn't you?" Mary laughed once she was lying down again.

"I guess so." Once her sister was situated, she picked up the bible again.

"Has he changed much?" The topic turned right back to Willis.

"Not so much physically. Mentally, I really think he has." Katie sat back down on the chair. "He didn't question why I was going to be baptized once; he used to question it all the time when we were younger." She smiled a little.

"Katie, are you in love?" The tone she used made her skin crawl. It felt like Mary was upset with her for almost moving on.

"Why would you say that?"

"You're blushing." Mary teased her now. "Come on, admit it. You like Willis."

"Do not." She felt a blush growing on her cheeks. "Do you want me to keep reading Leviticus or do you want some food?"

"Lunch sounds great, actually, Katie." Her sister smiled. "Do you know if mom has made any yet?"

"No, but I can go check. I might get roped into helping cook lunch, so I might be a while if she hasn't made it."

"I'll take a nap, then." She rested her head back on the pillows, letting it roll to the side. Her eyes closed, and Katie brushed some hair out of her face. She set the bible on the nightstand, and then began to walk downstairs.

The stairs creaked and refused to stay quiet. For Mary's sake, she hoped she was a heavy sleeper.

Once she was at the bottom of the stairs, Katie walked into the large summer kitchen. Her mom sat on a stool, canning a quart or so of ripe peaches.

"Mary's wondering about lunch, mom."

"You can make her something, Katie." Her mother didn't look up from canning. "Your father is out butchering the pig, and your grandparents are on the porch. See if they'd like any food. Your younger brothers and sister will be coming in with more peaches soon."

"Of course, mother." She smiled, and began to walk towards the porch. The large house made it a long walk. As she walked, she admired the well-made furniture. Her dad had made most of it by hand before she was born.

She opened the door to the porch and saw her grandmother and grandfather sitting on the bench.

"Grandma, grandpa, would you like some lunch?"

"That sounds wonderful, Katie." Her grandfather smiled, and her grandmother nodded. "Is it ready?"

"Not yet. I'll come get you when it is, though, grandpa." With that, she smiled. In this area of Pennsylvania, potatoes grew well. She decided to make a potato salad for the family, and began to gather potatoes to boil. Her mother had passed the recipe down to her last year, and the only way she would ever remember it was to make it often.

As she began to fill a pot with water, she thought about what Mary was doing. Her tone had become bitter at the end of the conversation they'd had, and she had felt rather uncomfortable. Why would Mary be so bitter?

Willis was two years older than she was. He'd often brushed her aside, not intentionally, but brushed aside all the same. As far as Katie was aware, Mary didn't even like Willis.

She sighed softly and turned the faucet off. The community here had gotten running water a few years ago, and it was such a relief. No longer did they have to warm the bath water by the stove or run outside to the pump every time they wanted water. They still used the pump, of course, to get water for the animals, but for them, they used the tap.

She set the pot of potatoes to boil as she heard the door open again. In came the rest of her siblings: Wayne, John, Samuel, and Hannah. Hannah was the youngest; at the tender age of 5, she could carry but only two peaches.

"Come here, Hannah." She smiled, and held her hands out for the peaches. Katie decided that a peach cobbler could make Mary feel a little better. "Wayne, how many peaches in that bucket?"

"Close to a hundred. How many more do you need?" Wayne was the eldest of the children, and had yet to marry. There were rumors that he was seeing a woman of 22 at the Sunday singings by the name Mary (no relation to his sister).

"Hannah's going to give me her two, so probably six or seven." As she spoke, she took the two peaches from her sister's hands gently. Wayne nodded and set the peaches on the counter.

"Peach cobbler sounds wonderful, Katie." He smiled at her before taking the rest of his peaches to the summer kitchen. Samuel and John followed suit, but did not stop to give her peaches. Hannah simply requested to mash the peaches; gladly, she peeled the peaches and put them in a bowl.

Then, she gave the bowl and a thick wooden dowel to Hannah.

"Mash away." She smiled and let her sister mash the peaches. Then, she checked on the potatoes for the salad. When they were soft, she pulled them out of the pot and began to mash them for the salad.

In all, it took her an hour to make the potato salad and stick the cobbler in the oven. She called everyone else into the kitchen and then put some on a plate for Mary.

"I'll take some up to Mary. Mom, the cobbler has about half an hour; could you pull it out when it's done?"

"I got it, Katie." John spoke up. "You take care of Mary." John was a year away from his *rumspringa*, but he had this certain quality of stubbornness. She doubted he'd be gone for long.

"Thank you." She smiled. "Tell grandma and grandpa I'm upstairs, please."

"Of course." With that, she walked two plates of potato salad up to Mary's room. Well, Mary shared it with her and Hannah. The three beds stretched east to west across the room, with a small closet to the other end of the beds. A nightstand was situated to the left of each bed for braiding strings and bibles. Flowers sometimes made it in, but that was rare.

"Mary?" Katie gently shook her sister awake. "Lunch is ready." She set one plate on the nightstand by her bed, and then she walked to hers.

"Mmm?" Mary never woke well, but today was a different story. "You made potato salad?"

"Yeah. Our potatoes haven't been stored right, so they were beginning to go bad." She began to eat her food. "There's a peach cobbler in the oven."

"Fresh peaches?"

"Yes, Mary. With fresh peaches; freshly picked this afternoon, actually."

"I guess that's what the others have been doing."

"Mom's been canning all morning, but yes. Our brothers and Hannah have been picking peaches all morning, they told me." She smiled, and watched as Mary ate her lunch in silence. The silence hurt a little bit; they were a tightly-knit community. What could be causing her to stop talking to her own sister? "Mary, did I do something wrong?"

"What do you mean?"

"You've hardly spoken a word to me other than to confirm your thoughts." She took another bite of her salad. "Did I do something wrong?"

"No. I'm very happy for you." There was a bitter tone. "Cross my heart."

"Alright..." Katie wasn't convinced, but let the topic drop. She finished her potato salad, and gathered up her dishes to take downstairs. "Are you done, Mary?"

"Yes." She almost shoved the plate at her, hardly touched. "I lost my appetite."

"Do you want some peach cobbler when it finishes?"

"No." Mary rolled over. "I'm going to finish my nap."

Katie didn't have time to object before Mary seemed to completely ignore her. She sighed softly and began to walk back downstairs. Maybe she could can some peaches before her cobbler finished.

She washed the dishes and put them away in silence. Tomorrow was Sunday; would she miss visiting and singing to take care of her sister?

Her mom came in as she was drying the plates, and picked up the utensils to dry.

"Do you want to go to the evening singing tomorrow night, Katie?" Her mom's question was a little on the nose. She nodded slowly. "Have you talked to Mary about it?"

"Mary won't talk to me." She tried not to cry. "She won't tolerate me for more than a few minutes at a time before she slips back into silence."

"When did this start?"

"This afternoon, after Willis visited." A tear trickled down her cheek, and she almost dropped the plates. Her mother took the plates and rag from her, setting them on the counter. Instead of wiping her tears away, she hugged her. Katie couldn't remember the last time her mother hugged her.

"It'll be alright, Katie. I think she's upset she can't go out into the world yet. She wants to spread her wings as badly as you did." Her mother rubbed her back as she found herself crying. "I know you haven't seen her in two years; it's natural to feel like there's a gap there."

She sniffled, eventually calming down.

"Thanks mom."

"Now, I think you should get the cobbler out. Enjoy a big piece." Her mother pulled away. "I'll finish the dishes."

She managed a smile and pulled the cobbler out. It was a little burnt on the edges, but her mother had saved it from burning too much by turning the oven off. Now, she set it on the cool counter on top of a small washcloth. Then, she began to cut the pieces. She cut it so that everyone could have a piece, though she cut Hannah's a little smaller so hers could be a little bigger.

Her mother laughed, but knew that's how they all did it. Whoever made the cobbler got the largest piece since Hannah was too young to have a normal sized piece yet. She managed a smile, and scooped a piece up for Mary. She carried it up the stairs, and then set it on Mary's nightstand. Even if she didn't want it now, she would have a piece available for her.

Then, she walked back downstairs to enjoy her piece. The rest of the family was coming in, and they all took a piece. They left the largest piece for her, an unspoken rule in the house.

"Thanks, Katie." Her grandmother smiled. "You're wonderful."

They ate the cobbler in silence. Her mind reeled, but she couldn't turn off the thoughts that her sister was bitter over Willis' attention to her.

***

Katie smiled as she put on her best clothes for the singing. It was almost six PM on Sunday evening, and her mother was going to help Mary for the night. Wayne and John were old enough to go to the singing events as well. Their grandparents would entertain Hannah and Samuel for the night.

"Are you ready, Katie?" Wayne called from the room across the hall.

"Almost, Wayne! I'll meet you at the door."

"Okay." Her brother left her alone and let her get ready in piece. She pulled her hair into a braid and quickly tied it off. She'd had enough of her hair being in her face, the stringy ends particularly.

Then, she walked downstairs. In her blue dress with long sleeves, slightly lower neckline but still appropriate, she felt as if she were going to catch Willis' attention again. Maybe it wouldn't be so bad, to have Willis paying attention to her. She did like him quite a bit, but wasn't sure she would like to marry him.

Based on their interactions earlier, however, she knew that it'd be a good choice to marry him. He'd blossomed into a young Amish man that no woman would be able to say no to.

With that thought tucked away in her head, she arrived at the door. Wayne and John were already there, both dressed in their best clothes. Their mother waited to see them off.

"I'll take good care of Mary tonight, Katie. Enjoy your night." Her words made Katie smile. "If she wants you here, I'll come get you, but I hope you get to enjoy the night." With that, she sent them off towards the barn where Sunday evening singing was held every week.

It was a silent, ten minute walk. The silence was not like those that Mary forced upon her. Instead, the silence filled her with hope and joy; this would be quite an exciting night. She would have a chance to see other members of the community that she hadn't seen, and possibly find someone who struck her fancy.

When they arrived at the barn, the singing was up and running already. She separated from her brothers, promising to find them at the end of the event. They smiled, nodded, and agreed to it. Then, they proceeded to join in on the festivities. A long table with food sat to one side of the barn.

She migrated over to see if someone had brought cherry cobbler. While her family didn't grow cherries, plenty of other families did. The table had plenty of finger foods, and two cherry cobblers sat to one side. One had already been half eaten, and the other was untouched. She cut herself a small slice of cherry cobbler and began to eat it.

"Katie?" A voice behind her made her jump; she almost lost her cherry cobbler. She turned around, and laid eyes on Willis.

"Willis." She smiled after swallowing. "I didn't expect to see you here today."

"I could say the same thing about you." He smiled back. "Is Mary doing better?"

"Mom's watching her tonight so I could come here. If I'm needed at home, someone else will come to get me." She smiled a little more. "Your baptism was a lovely service."

"Thank you." He couldn't help but grin at her with his goofy, toothy smile. "I hope your baptism service is as lovely." She felt her cheeks heating up a little.

"Is there a reason you wanted to talk to me, Willis?" She took another bite of her cherry cobbler. Cherry juices ran down her chin, and she managed to catch them with a napkin.

"Would you like to meet up next week at the evening singing?" He handed her another napkin as he asked. She almost choked on her cobbler.

"M-Me?" She couldn't believe his words. "You want to meet up with me next week?"

"Yes." His smile turned into a slight frown. "Do you not want to?"

"N-No, I want to." She managed another smile. "I didn't think you'd ask so soon."

"Wonderful!" He smiled, a little too excited. "I hope you don't mind that it was so soon."

"No, not at all." Her voice quivered a little. "I'm worried about how Mary will react, though." Willis' brows furrowed. "Mary's been giving me the silent treatment."

"Why?"

"I don't know." She sighed, and picked a plate up to set her cobbler on. "I think it has to do with your visit yesterday. It didn't start until after you visited."

"I only visited to say hello." His brows stayed furrowed. "I didn't mean to make her think I was interested in anyone unwillingly..."

"She teased me about it before we went on *rumspringa*. Now, she teases with a bitter tone and a scornful eye." She sighed, dabbing at her cherry stained lips. "She won't even hold a conversation with me beyond making sure she knows what's going on."

"Do you think she wanted me?"

"I think it's because her *rumspringa* was delayed. She's a lot like you were before you left, Willis." She took another bite of her cobbler as the rest of the group started another song. "She wants to leave the community for good."

"I don't think she'll want to after she spends some time out in the real world." He cut himself a piece of cobbler as he spoke. "I thought I wanted to, and then I realized that it was nothing without the community. Without you." He flashed her a smile before he took a bite of his cobbler.

"Without me?" She found herself blushing again. The heat in her cheeks told her so.

He nodded slowly as he swallowed.

"Without you, I found that the women wanted to be with me. Apparently, I'm a good looker. Until they realize I won't be able to pay for everything they want, at least." He laughed. "All the girls I met wanted money."

"A lot of guys I met simply wanted me on their arm for a pretty face." She sighed, rolling her eyes. "I hated it. Eventually, I gave up and started saying no to them. One of them had ties to a gang, and...and they almost killed me. That's why I came home." In the middle of her story, her tone changed. She felt tears welling in her eyes, but she refused to cry.

"I'm sorry to hear that, Katie." Willis put a hand on her shoulder softly. "I think it was smart to come back home after that."

"Mary broke her leg the next week, and we had to postpone my baptism." She pushed tears out of her eyes softly, trying not to make it obvious that she wanted to cry.

"Katie?" A voice interrupted the conversation. "Mary's asking for you at home." Looking around, she found Samuel standing in front of her. "Mom sent me."

"Thanks, Samuel. I'll walk you home." She cut another piece of cherry cobbler before she turned to Willis. "I'll see you around, Willis."

"See you around, Katie." He smiled at her, and gave her a small wink before she led her younger brother out of the room. "I'll tell your brothers that you had to go early." She smiled.

"Thanks." With that, they left the singing and began to walk back to their home.

"Can I have a bite, Katie?"

"That's why I cut another piece, Sam." She smiled, and used a fork to cut a small bite off for her brother. "Here you go."

"Thanks!" Her brother's face lit up, and she couldn't help but smile as he took a bite of the cobbler. "Cherry?"

"Yes. I don't know who made it, but it's good, isn't it?" She took another bite after she finished speaking.

"Yes." Her brother smiled. "Are you okay?"

"Willis and I were having a conversation about our time outside the community."

"Oh. Is it hard for you to talk about?"

"At times." She smiled a little. "Tonight was one of those times, but it had nothing to do with you or Willis."

"Did you enjoy the time with Willis?"

"Yes." She smiled, brushing a loose strand of her hair behind her ear. "I did."

"Should we expect a wedding soon?" Samuel began to tease her. "Willis and Katie getting married?"

"Samuel!" She half-scolded him, but the laugh in her voice gave her away. "I don't know." She sighed. "I honestly don't know. You know relationships are never public until a wedding date is for sure."

"I know." He sighed now. "Can I have another piece?"

"Fork?" She held her hand out for his fork as they neared the porch of their house. He happily handed her the fork, and she gave him another piece. "Thank you, Katie."

"You're welcome. Share the rest of that piece with mom and Hannah, okay?"

"Okay!" He took the plate and forks before heading towards their parents' bedroom.

"And with dad if he's home." She called after him, and only got a thumbs-up in the air. She laughed, and then headed upstairs to her room. Mary was fast asleep in her bed. As quietly as she could, she changed into something she could sleep in. Hannah was not asleep yet.

"Katie, is that you?" Mary softly spoke.

"Yes. Did I wake you?"

"No." She rolled away from her. "You can go back to the singing."

"But Sam said..." She was unsure of what to do; now half changed into something to sleep in, she couldn't go back.

"Mom had to go do something; I'm fine." The bitter tone returned. "Go away."

"Mary, we have to talk about this." She pulled her sleeping clothes on the rest of the way and sat down at the head of Mary's bed. "Why are you being so bitter?"

"Did Willis ask you to meet him next week?"

"What?"

"Did Willis ask you to meet him next week?" Her sister repeated the question, but didn't look at her.

"Yes." She softly answered. "But he didn't mean to upset you yesterday."

"I thought you were going to wait until I was out to do that!" Mary almost exploded at her.

"What?"

"I thought you were going to wait until I was in the world to do that." She sniffled. "No one ever seems to care what I think!"

"Mary, that's not true, and you know it." She touched her sister's shoulder. "What do you think?"

"I want to go out." Her sister's voice quivered. "I want to be independent." At this, Katie crossed the room to face her sister. Tears streamed down her cheeks, and she was sobbing too hard to say anything.

Katie simply hugged her tightly, unsure of how to take the new development. However, the hug didn't last long. Mary pushed her away hard, sending her to the floor. She sat up slowly, her head spinning lightly.

"What was that for?" She tried not to sound upset with her sister, but failed.

"Hugging me!" Mary now yelled at her. "I don't like being touched."

"I'm sorry. I thought you could use a hug." She sincerely apologized. "Are you okay?"

"What?"

"Are you okay, Mary?" She sat on her knees, closer to the bed. "Emotionally, are you okay?"

Her sister sniffled, confused by the question. She let her sister take her time, hoping that their parents hadn't heard Mary yelling.

"I-I...I'm okay now." She sniffled again, wiping her eyes. "Do you think you'll marry him, Katie?"

"I don't know." She smiled a little. "Please, don't tell anyone."

"I won't." Her sister sniffled again. She handed her a napkin, and waited as Mary blew her nose. "I think you two make a good couple."

"Are you done ignoring me?"

"Ignoring you?"

"You weren't doing it on purpose?"

"No. I wasn't sure why you were the one watching me so often." Her sister propped herself up on her elbow, careful of putting extra weight on her broken leg.

"Because I love you, Mary." She smiled softly. "Everyone else has been helping can."

"You don't really like to can, I remember now."

"Yup." She laughed a little as she remembered the incident that had turned her off of canning. Her finger had gotten stuck in a jar or a lid – she couldn't ever quite remember which – and had been covered by scalding fruit. Her finger was still scarred from it.

"I'm sorry, Katie." She spoke in a soft voice. "I didn't mean to tear you away from the singing."

"It's alright, Mary." She squeezed her sister's hand lightly before pulling away. "Why don't you get some rest?"

"The peach cobbler was delicious, by the way." Her sister smiled. "Thank you."

"You're welcome." She smiled. Maybe this would end well after all.

***

A month and a half later, Katie stood in her room, wearing a simple blue dress with a big bunch of flowers in her hands. The weekend after Willis had asked to see her the next week, he drove her home. Wayne and John left them alone to talk, having left earlier in the evening.

Willis had made the journey to his house at two in the morning, and their friendship acted as a catalyst. It was the quickest courtship they had seen in the community in decades, her grandmother said.

"Katie?" Hannah's voice filtered up the stairs. She turned around, and saw her youngest sibling sitting on the top stair. "You wove Willis?"

"Yes. I love Willis." She smiled, and picked up her younger sister. "One day, you too will be in love. It won't be for years, but it will be soon."

"Ew." She made a face. "Me no wove boys!" Katie laughed.

"Do you like my dress?" She quickly distracted her sister.

"I do!" She smiled widely. "Katie wook pretwy!" She laughed again.

"Do you want to wear a blue dress too, Hannah?" When her sister nodded excitedly, she set her down on the bed and looked for Hannah's blue dress. She found it under the bed, and helped her younger sister change.

Mary had left to explore the outside world the week before, but was returning to see her sister get married. She would be wearing something from the outside world – a dress, she believed it was, in a greenish color.

She shook her head lightly and began to braid Hannah's hair as she hummed a hymn. They still had about an hour before the wedding was to begin. They would make visits next weekend, since they had church tomorrow. Due to the timing of the year, they were able to get married quickly.

"Is Hannah up there with you, Katie?" Her mother's voice came up the stair case.

"Yes, mother." She smiled. "She's with me."

"Katie wook pwetty!" Her sister again complimented her, pronouncing the word 'pretty' differently than she had before. It was all part of a five year old's charm, though.

"Okay; I wanted to make sure she hadn't run off. Willis will be here soon; are you ready?"

"I'm ready. I didn't think he'd be here for another hour..."

"He's going to be early." Her mother did not hesitate to say it. "He told me last night that he wanted to see you before the wedding, but I asked him not to come so early."

"It's alright, mom. Is everyone else here?"

"Everyone's early, oddly enough. When he gets here, we can start." When she said that, her nerves began to jump. She was really doing this; she was really getting married.

The door downstairs opened, and she heard her to-be husband's voice in the hallway. She sent Hannah down ahead of her, her braid wildly flinging against the air as she ran. Katie took in a deep breath, and then began to walk downstairs.

The ceremony was all that she had hoped it would be. Mary had brought a friend with her – a guy who thought he was falling in love with her. They spent an entire afternoon singing, dancing, and enjoying the community's company. For the moment, they were to stay with her family until their new house was finished. The community was going to help them work on it tomorrow, so it shouldn't take long at all.

At the end of the festivities, Katie essentially collapsed in Willis' arms. Mary and her friend had driven home. Everyone else was getting ready to go; they had a long buggy ride ahead of them to get back to her place. Willis placed a soft kiss on her forehead before helping her up and out to the buggy.

"I love you." He spoke the words first. They had yet to say them to each other, but in the quiet of the night in the buggy, he broke the silence with them.

"I love you too, Willis." She couldn't help but feel an overwhelming smile on her face. A sense of belonging took over her, and she rested her head on his chest as they began the ride home. It was difficult to find a comfortable position in the bouncing buggy. Sleeping would have to wait until they arrived home.

"Are you looking forward to having a family?" He again spoke up.

"Yes." She couldn't stop her smile from widening. "I want to have a large family. Five kids, at least."

"Five kids, at least, it is." He smiled and laughed. "It sounds wonderful. And on our farm, what shall we grow?"

"Cherries, peaches, potatoes, and anything else you can think of." She smiled. "I can farm, and you can put your carpenter skills to good use."

"Good thing I have my own tools." Another chuckle came from his mouth. It shook his chest under her, and she smiled. The silence set in again, but it was a good, comfortable type. She bit her lip softly, and pressed her head against his shoulder. He put an arm around her, drawing her closer to him on the seat.

Before she could object, he had a blanket out from under the seat and laid it across the both of them.

"Better?" He smiled down at her.

"Much, thank you." She couldn't hide her smile, even if she wanted to. "Can I fall asleep now?"

"We're almost there, Katie." He brushed some of the loose hair out of her face. "But I will carry you in if you fall asleep."

"I love you so much." Her words echoed softly in the dark night, and she closed her eyes. His arms held her closer, and she could feel the buggy bounce up and down under them.

As she was falling asleep, the buggy came to a sudden, jerky stop. Willis stopped her from falling off the bench, and picked her up.

"But I'm not asleep..."

"I want to carry you in." He smiled down at her. "Sleep. We can always talk tomorrow. You're exhausted."

"Thank you." She smiled, speaking softly. He opened the door and walked her inside. She closed her eyes again, and found herself quickly drifting off to sleep. She felt him carry her up the stairs. He set her on the bed, and she heard him shuffling about the room for a few moments.

He got in bed beside her, and she felt a different kind of material touch her skin. He'd changed clothes before he got in with her. She smiled, and drifted off into a wonderful sleep.

amish awakening

Chapter 1

Hannah stood at the window of her classroom looking out towards the green landscape that stretched out as far as she could see, dark clouds started gathering and was drawing closer with each passing minute. To most those clouds were a sign of new life, but to her it bore nothing but bad memories she simply chose to forget. Father Smith often told her that in order to find peace within herself she would need to make peace with herself, but how could she if it wasn't herself she was angry at? It wasn't her fault that Aaron died.

"Hanna, will you be fine to get home before the storm gets here?" Kemp asked as popping his head in at the class.

Kemp had been a good friend for her, since Aaron's death he had taken it upon himself to be the man of the house, but as Aaron's younger sibling, she felt awkward knowing that he wanted more from her. He may not have said it out loud but his constant fussing over her wellbeing said enough.

"I'll be fine, thank you Kemp, I'm having supper with Father Smith and his family," she said and offered him a friendly smile.

"Of course, well you be careful now," Kemp said and hesitated before turning to leave.

Hannah let out a soft sigh and sent up a silent prayer of thanks. She was growing weary trying to be nice all the time by courteously ignoring Kemp's advances, but some days she itched to just be blatantly rude and tell him to stop trying. But that will cause a few frowns to furrow on the elders' brows. She waited until Kemp was out of sight before she grabbed her basket with her books and left the single structured school building that housed no more than thirty four school children ranging from all ages.

She hurried along the road to get home but the storm was drawing closer faster than expected. Another perfect day ruined, she thought as she treaded ahead, keeping a watchful eye on the clouds rolling in and as the first drops started plummeting down on her she quickened her pace. The sound of rolling thunder droned in her ears and she clutched her basket tighter, but when an automobile pulled up next to her she realized it was not thunder.

"You won't make it far at this pace *lieb*," the very familiar yet disembodied voice of the driver spoke from inside the car.

"*Lieb*? It is a bad habit making such a personal reference to complete stranger," she said to the man and stepped closer to get a better look at her assailant or her rescuer.

"Greetings Hannah, it's been a long time."

Hannah froze; it was Mason who sat before her as big as life, in an automobile of all things. The last time she had seen him was when she was just seventeen. He had always been the black sheep in the community, disobeying so many of the rules, that by the time he turned eighteen he decided to venture into the great big modern world, and disappeared from her life.

"Mason Smith," she said and smiled, "you have not changed one bit."

He threw his head back and laughed, "In this light you cannot see my grey hairs. Now are you going to walk the rest of the way home, or will you let me take you."

She swayed and looked down at her feet, contemplating a ride. She was sure that it will just loosen a few tongues if she arrived home with him.

"*Denki*, but I think I will walk, it's not too far now," she declined and stepped away from the automobile, "I'm sure to see you at your father's house?"

Mason smiled and nodded at her, "That depends if my father will welcome me into his house."

"The Prodigal son returns," she said raising her shoulders and tucking them forward as the rain started to pelt down around her, "I'll see you later."

Instead of running along the road, she chose to run across the fields towards her house and away from Mason. Seeing him after all these years should not have caused such a kaleidoscope of butterflies to wreak havoc in her stomach but it has. She had noticed the slight grey hair peppered against his temples and the increased amount of laughing lines that deepened next to his eyes when he smiled. He had also no beard, which meant that he had not yet been wed, but then again, the modern worlds' cultures are far different to their own simple way of life, and the mere thought left her wondering where he had been all these years.

By the time she reached her house, she was completely drenched right through to her undergarments. She suddenly felt nervous to attend supper with the Smiths' but unless she was ill she could not come up with an honest enough excuse as to why she can't attend. She was going to have to just try and act as normal as possible around Mason, that is if his father allows him to sit with them.

Chapter 2

Mason left the community just after his eighteenth birthday, and the day he left, his father told him that he would wait for him. Personally he never thought he would come back here, but life has the tendency to throw curveballs when least expected. And from personal experience the curve balls just keep coming.

He hardly expected to see Hannah, or rather he expected that she would still be here, but he didn't expect their run in with each other to have such an effect on him. Even when he approached her from a distance, his gut told him that it was Hannah walking alongside the road. Call it providence or pure chance, but he would recognize her from every angle simply by the way she walked. She had this distinct way of walking on her toes while hardly moving her arms. Now years after experiencing the modern world, her walk reminded him a ballerina, precise and delicately calculated and all his memories came flooding back.

When she ran across the field he couldn't help but smile, knowing that she too had a moment of dejavu and for a moment he silently wished he never left, but he knew if he did stay it would have been for her only and he simply could not tie himself down to a life of common needs and simplicity, he was too eager to explore the world.

As he pulled up to his fathers' house he looked up at the house, as usual well kept, but a simple uncomplicated structure, like their way of life here in Lancaster. He remembered his life here as if it was yesterday, and although he had an enquiring and curious mind, he had to admit that staying here would have prevented many complications in his life. His cell phone vibrated on his dash but he chose to ignore it, instead he shoved it in the glove compartment and got out of the car.

"Mason!" his mother cried out as she came running down the stairs hugging him tight.

His father stood at the stop of the stairs with his arms crossed and a deadpan expression that would put a corpse to shame, but then again his father was never one to show any emotion unless it was to hand out corporal punishment and of that he had more than his fair share.

"*Mamm*, it's good to see you," he said and hugged his mother. She had gotten old and although she appeared relaxed he could see that life and labour had taken its toll.

"Mason my son, please come inside, we are so happy to have you here," his mother said excitedly.

"*Daed*, how are you?" he asked his father boldly.

"We're fine, ya," his father responded flatly and stood aside for him to enter.

Nothing had changed since he initially left for his Rumspringa, which he never returned from, and being back after so many years, was like a time traveling experience.

"Lydia is married now," his mom said as she set a space for him at the dinner table.

"I know, she wrote me."

His mother and father exchanged looks and then went on as if he never said a word.

"She's with child, and the baby should be here within the month or so."

Clearly his father did not approve of his sister writing to him, so instead he smiled, "I will make an effort to congratulate her when I see her."

The awkward silence was followed with a light knock and when he turned around to see who it was, he was pleasantly surprized to find Hannah standing in the doorway.

"Mason, Hannah has dinner with us every Friday evening," his mother said and gestured for Hannah to sit down.

Mason turned to her, "Do you not have a family of your own?"

"Let's say grace," Mason's father interrupted and he immediately could have kicked himself for asking such a personal question. Now that he was back among his family he had to be careful of what he said and how he said things.

They all took hands and while his father said grace, Mason was acutely aware of Hannah's hand in his. He could feel her fingers trembling in his and he smiled. He made her nervous; he could only hope it was the good kind of nervous.

After dinner they all sat at the table while Hannah and Mrs Smith gathered the dishes and took it to the kitchen.

"How long are you planning on visiting?" Mason's father asked.

"Not sure, at the moment it's indefinitely."

A loud crash sounded from the kitchen, and his father's intense gaze held his.

"Indefinitely is a long time."

"Depending on the inevitability of it," Mason said.

"You're room is still as it was, your mother never changed it. She waited for you."

"At least someone did."

He held his father's gaze and then stood up and excused himself. He had to give his father time; he had been away for such a long time, with little or no contact. But then again if they were just a little bit more open minded towards the use of modern technology he would have been in constant contact with his family. The few letters he exchanged with his sister was hard enough to keep up with, as it stands, people no longer wrote letters and wasted their time with postage, they e-mailed or chatted to each other.

"I'll get my things from the car," Mason said and excused himself from the table.

Chapter 3

Hannah spent the entire evening seated next to Mason trying her best not to breathe, or inhale the intoxicating smell that filled her nostrils every time he moved. The odd time she visited town she often took a sneaky sniff of the perfumes that were sold, more to remind her just how much power there was in such an evil cheap substance, or so she told herself. But now here next to Mason, the smell turned from offensive to hallucinogenic. Every time she found herself leaning towards him and then she had to recite a bible verse that reminded her of infidelity and the sinful nature of the flesh. I shall not want, she kept saying to herself mentally and when Mrs Smith got up and started to clear the table, she was only too thankful to join her and get away from the magnetic pull that was threatening to ruin her.

That was until she heard Mason mention that his stay was indefinite. That meant she was going to see him every single day until he decides to run away again.

The words came as such a shock that she dropped the plate she was holding. Mrs Smith was quick to bend down and help her pick up the broken pieces.

"He has changed," she said to Hannah, "but he's still my son."

"The world tends to change a person," Hannah whispered and smiled at the older woman with the sad blue eyes.

She remembered the day they realized Mason was not going to come back, his mother was in tears for days, while his father put up this façade of callous indifference. But she knew they missed their son.

"Hannah, you can make him see the truth."

That was a tall order; Hannah thought and tossed the glass into the bin.

"I don't think it is my place to convince him," she said.

"You're right I'm sorry, I just – I don't want him to leave again."

Hannah could understand how Mason's mother must have felt, for someone to leave for such a long time is almost like sending someone off to the beyond. But how was she going to convince him to stay, he had experienced the modern world and drove an automobile not to mention that he used men's perfume. Why would he trade that freedom for this?

"I think I need to head home Mrs Smith, I still have a quilt to finish before Sunday," she said and gathered her coat, "I'll be seeing you."

"Of course dear, but do come around when you want some company."

"I sure will."

Hannah was tucked under her blanket in front of the fireplace and had just started to quilt when there was a slight knock on the door. What a strange time for a visitor, she thought as she went to open the door.

"Mason," she said shocked.

"Hannah, may I come in?"

"I-I don't think it's proper for me to invite you in," she said and reached for her shawl, and then stepped outside, closing the door behind her.

"I understand, I just thought you could use some company," he said with a smile that tugged at the corners of his mouth.

She felt her stomach tumble again and she took a deep steadying breath.

"We can go for a walk," she offered.

"Sure." Mason held out his arm but instead she wrapped her arms around herself.

"Why did you come back?"

"It's a long story."

One he would most likely not want to share with her, but she was curious as to why he was back. What if he was running from the law, she thought slightly panicked, but she couldn't see him to be someone who would use this community as a curtain to hide behind.

"We'll time is what I have. You left here in such a hurry, and now after I don't know even how long, you're back like a ghost from the past."

"Maybe I am a ghost, and I decided to come and haunt you," he said and laughed.

Hannah also laughed and shook her head, "A lot has changed since you left."

"Like what, a few more babies born and a few sad souls sent to the hereafter? Come on Hannah, nothing changes amongst the Amish, you know that."

"Well I got married," she said and when he stopped she turned to look at him.

"And you're here walking with me, what will your husband have to say?"

"He's no longer here; he passed away," *and I'm grateful he did*, she thought not voicing her true feelings. What would Mason have said if he knew Aaron's true colours?

"So who was he?"

"Who was who?"

"Your husband, who was the lucky guy?"

"Aaron."

An awkward silence settled between them and Hannah bit her lip. Even when they were teenagers, Mason and Aaron always competed to gain her attention. They were the trio of friends who did everything together as kids, and as they got older she always thought she would marry Mason the day they were old enough. But the day Mason left he broke her heart, she waited for him to return but he never did and eventually she gave in and married Aaron, thinking they would have a happy life. But Aaron wasn't the same fun loving boy she knew or maybe he knew all along that he was just a plaster for her broken heart, a replacement for Mason, which is why he was so angry with her all the time.

"Was he good to you?" Mason asked as if he could read her mind.

"He was a good man," she responded averting her eyes.

"That was not my question Hannah," he said and took her by the shoulders, "was he good to you?"

In the moonlight she could see the flecks of silver in his blue eyes, and her heart ached with longing. But this was not right, no matter what her heart and body wanted, in her mind she was determined that she would not lust after another man. Yes she was a widow and yes, she may remarry, but that thought had never crossed her mind. Only now with Mason back she had dabbled with the idea of having her happily ever after, but it was only a dream. Just like the dream she had when she was only sixteen. And from experience all dreams eventually fade and turn into a cruel reality.

She pulled away from him and turned around to head back to the house.

"I do not wish to discuss Aaron with you," she blurted out as she felt tears sting her eyes, "Go home Mason, your mother will be worried about you."

Chapter 4

Mason had this strange feeling that Aaron had turned out to be exactly what he always thought. As young men they both loved Hannah, and although they never showed it in the open there was a sort of rivalry between them. The day he decided to go on a Rumspringa, Aaron had thanked him for leaving, and Mason had felt as if he had betrayed Hannah, but Aaron was also his friend and at the time he figured he'll be the lesser one and allow his friend a fair chance, hoping that Hannah will calm the anger in Aaron. Aaron was your average young man, but he had an angry and cruel disposition, when no-one was watching he was the one who threw stones at new born lambs and shot birds out of the trees with a sling shot, simply for the fun of it. Even his mother had to deal with his insubordination, but in front of the rest of the community he was the son everyone wished for.

Mason felt a cold stab of regret at the thought of Aaron hurting Hannah and knowing that he was indirectly to blame, made him feel sick. He had to find out what she had gone through and try and fix what he had broken, but with the hands of time waiting for no one, he wouldn't even know where to start, or whether it was too late for a new beginning.

He set off after Hannah as she rushed back to the house.

"Hannah wait!" he called but she didn't turn, she just walked straight ahead.

"Hannah!"

"Go home Mason," she said sternly but as she reached for the door handle he placed his hand over hers.

"Did he hurt you?"

He felt her back straighten and her entire body go rigid, her actions confirming his suspicions.

"Oh my god, I'm so sorry," he said and squeezed her shoulder with his other hand.

She turned in his arms and her eyes were cold and hard as she looked at him.

"Do not use the Lords name in vain."

Right, he was among very religious people now, he had to count his words and check his actions all the time.

"I'm sorry, it's a bad habit, but I am truly sorry," he said and then pulled her in to hug her.

"Mason, please," he heard her plead against his chest, "why don't you go back to where you came from?"

Was she so mad at him that she wanted him to leave? He knew he probably didn't deserve her time but surely she could understand that they were all young and he was curious about the world. She could have gone with him when he asked her but she was too scared to set foot outside of this protected cocoon of a life she was too familiar with.

"That's not happening in a hurry sweetheart," he said and tilted her chin up, "I'm here to stay, for a while."

When she looked up at him he was tempted to kiss her, but instead he took a step back.

"I'll be seeing you at Church on Sunday," he said and then tipped his hat and made his way home.

He had to keep reminding himself that life amongst the Amish wasn't anything like the world out there; he had to watch his tongue and try his best not to be tempted by a beautiful woman. As it were, temptation had caused him enough headaches to last him a life time.

He looked at his phone and grimaced. Roxanne had been phoning him non-stop, and he had no desire to return her calls and if he had a penny left he would pay her to go away. She deceived him, made him believe she was in love with him, and then tricked him into making him believe she was with child. He had found out by chance that she was lying to him, and when he did it was the last straw. It was that, which finally made him realize that the world he had chosen to embrace was nothing but a place where people are self-centred and illogical. None of his worldly friends or rather foes knew where he was, he had also turned off his location based service on his phone in case anyone wanted to track him down.

If he was going to make a change and revert back to the old ways of the Amish, he was going to have to consider getting rid of his electronic devices, but he wasn't so sure if he was willing to part with his music. That was the one thing he had grown to enjoy about life on the outside, while here amongst the Amish musical instruments were forbidden.

Chapter 5

A week has passed since Mason's arrival in Lancaster, and Hannah had done everything in her power to avoid him. Not because she disliked him or because she was angry with him, but because he stirred emotions she had completely forgotten about. She spent hours on her knees praying that the Lord take away the feelings that she harboured.

She glanced at herself in the mirror once again and sighed. Why does she even bother about her appearance, it was not like her to be so vain, but she's spent more time in front of the mirror in the past week than she did in her entire life. She rolled her plated hair into a bun and pinned it to her head before putting on her bonnet, she had to get over this stupid notion that there could be anything between her and Mason. He was a confused man with a foot in both worlds, and if he was not able to decide where he belonged how was she going to fit into his world anyway. Tonight she was going to be attending the sing, and she knew for a fact that Mason would be there too. Her stomach tumbled again and she clutched the front of her dress and sighed heavily. The sooner she got this over with the better, but as she exited the house, he was waiting for her. He had borrowed his father's buggy and was even wearing traditional Amish clothes.

"I was about to come and find you," he said and smiled.

"You wouldn't have had to look far."

"Indeed, you look beautiful."

Hannah felt her cheeks flame up and she quickly looked down and cleared her throat. Why after all these years did he still have this effect on her?

"Thank you."

"Can I offer you a ride to the Sing?"

"I was- I was going to take a walk, I enjoy the fresh air," she lied and shifted her weight.

"Are you going to avoid me for the rest of your life?"

"I don't know what you mean."

"You avoided me at church service; you hide in your class room every day. I'm not a bad man Hannah," he said and came to stand before her.

"I'm not avoiding you, I'm a busy woman," *and dead scared that the feelings I have will be unrequited,* she thought.

"Lying is as great a sin as blasphemy, so why don't you tell me why you are avoiding me?"

Hannah rolled her eyes and stepped past him, "We're going to be late, and I don't have time for idle chit chat."

"We're not going anywhere until you tell me what you are afraid of," he insisted and caught her arm.

She felt a shiver run down her spine as his hand wrapped around her upper arm, and although her sleeve offered some resistance it still felt as if his fingers were touching her bare skin.

Should she tell him what really scared her, and admit to him that she still had feelings for him despite the fact that she had given herself to Aaron all those years ago? Should she tell him how Aaron took his anger outbursts out on her and caused her to lose their child? The day she was promised to Aaron her nightmare started, although she could not deny him physically she hated every intimate moment with him. He took what he wanted when he wanted, and if she wasn't responsive enough he would get physically abusive with her. It took her a good few years to finally get over her fears and make peace with what had happened. The community never spoke a word about it although they all knew, and even when the elders got involved nothing was done.

"Get in the buggy, I'll take you to the sing," he said and led her to the carriage.

"It's not appropriate," she said and tugged her arm free.

"We're adults, not teenagers," he said and then softened his tone, "It's just a ride to my father's house."

She sighed and then got into the buggy, with her hands folded tightly on her lap.

The drive to the sing was cloaked in complete silence, and it felt as if she was suffocating with words that were trying to force their way up in her throat. She had to just get through this evening and keep calm, she kept telling herself, but she knew that it was not going to be that easy. Mason kept looking at her and she could feel his gaze rest on her face.

"Staring at me is not going to change anything," she said and looked directly at him. If he wasn't going to get the hint she was going to have to be honest with him.

He pulled the carriage to a halt and turned to her and unexpectedly cupped her face and pressed his lips against hers. For a moment she froze as his lips pressed against hers, then suddenly that intoxicated musky scent filled her senses. Her defences weakened instantly and she willingly parted her lips, but as his tongue touched hers she pulled away and jumped out of the buggy and ran.

"Lord, forgive me, I have sinned," she prayed and rushed across the field towards the Smiths' house. How could she have been so weak to allow a man to seduce her? But even as guilt flooded her, she kept thinking of his kiss and memories of a long time ago flooded her mind.

The day before he left he had kissed her, not like he kissed her tonight, but it was a kiss that remained with her all these years. A kiss she tucked away in the confines of her mind, and now that, that memory had resurfaced she felt confused and uncertain.

By the time she got to the Sing, Mason's carriage was already there. She composed herself as much as she could before entering the house. He was nowhere to be seen, but the house was full of young eager teenagers, happily singing their songs of worship. Although the event had nothing to do with devotion it was one of the more sociable events, where all the young people normally got to socialize.

She made her way through to the kitchen and joined the older women where they were preparing food.

"Did Mason fetch you?" Mrs Smith asked as she came to stand next to Hannah.

"He did come around, but I walked here instead," she said softly.

"He fancies you Hannah," she said as she moved closer, almost whispering.

"I know, I just don't know if it's appropriate. He hasn't been among us for so long and people will talk."

"You're a widow, Aaron is gone and I can guarantee you that no one will be raising any brows at you."

Hannah sighed, if it wasn't Mason it was his mother, but she knew that someone in the community would have something to say about such a union.

During the sing, Hannah was intensely aware of Mason's presence, but what made it worst was that Kemp was also there, and it suddenly felt like a bad case of dejavu with a very familiar love triangle forming, but Kemp was not aware of Mason's intent. Sooner or later he was going to realize it and then she would be stuck in the middle.

Before the sing was over, she snuck out, hoping that she left undetected, but her luck had run out.

"Hannah," it was Kemp who fell into step beside her, "You're leaving so early, are you not feeling well?"

"Oh no, I'm fine, I'm just a little tired."

She was lying again, she was going to go straight to hell at this rate, she thought to herself.

"Let me get the carriage and I'll take you home."

"No!" she all but shouted, and then toned her voice down, "I mean, no thank you. I'd rather walk."

The look on Kemp's face was one of concern but he didn't push, he simply smiled, "I'll keep you company then."

She was growing weary with this whole avoiding men thing, at this point she felt as if she was a lamb being cornered by a pack of wolves and she hated every minute of it. On the one hand Kemp was a nice man, the complete opposite of Aaron, but he was just too familiar to her. And then there was Mason, who she had feelings for since the age of fourteen. This was all too much.

"Hannah, we've known each other for a long time, and I was thinking we should consider a future together," he said out of the blue.

"Uh-I, I'm not sure I understand?"

"I want to marry you," Kemp said without blinking.

If she had a mouth full of food, she would have choked right this minute. This was a little sudden, and she knew why he had moved so quickly, he must feel threatened with Mason back in town.

"Kemp, you're a wonderful man, but I don't see a future with you, we've had too much history and having been married to Aaron makes it awkward."

"How so?" he asked as he took her hand in his.

She pulled her hand away, "It just does, if I was to marry again, it would be for love and what we have is just a friendship, which I value."

The disappointment on his face saddened her, but she could not lie and pretend that she saw a future with him. She stood and watched as he finally walked away from her before she continued to her house, but as she reached her door, Mason appeared out of the shadows.

"So it's Kemp?" he asked blankly.

"Excuse me?"

"Kemp, you wouldn't even allow me to take you to the sing because you don't want him to see you with me."

"First of all, it is not Kemp, we are just friends and secondly the reason I walked to the sing was because you kissed me. You had no right," she said angrily.

"You enjoyed that kiss as much as I did, why do you deny it?"

Hannah unlocked her door and then turned to Mason, "This is not a forsaken place like the city Mason, we have values, I have values and if you cannot respect that then there is no place for you here."

Mason approached her and stopped so close she could inhale his very breath.

"Do you have feelings for me, because if you don't, I need to know and stop wasting my time."

"Why? It's not as if you're planning on staying here, you'll leave just like you did all those years ago and I'm sorry Mason, but I will not subject myself to such disappointment again."

She didn't wait for his response simply entered the house and shut the door behind her. Regardless of the condition of her heart, she was not going to leave it out in the open to be trampled on again. The ball was in his court now, if he really was interested in her. He would have to prove himself.

Chapter 6

Mason spent a week contemplating his future, and every time he saw Hannah, he was more and more convinced that he would not leave a second time, and after consulting with his father and the other elders, they agreed to baptize him into the church. He may have been gone longer than most, but he was never officially shunned from the community. And regardless of his life style in the city, they opted to overlook his error in judgement.

It was a private affair with only the elders and his close family around to witness the baptism, and once it was over, he decided to go to the school and wait for Hannah. When she exited the school his heart skipped a beat, it was quite strange how his own emotions were suddenly so intensified after the baptism, he had often wondered if this baptism really changed anyone, but now he knew beyond the shadow of a doubt he was a new person. He had died down his old life and was willing to walk the straight and narrow with Hannah by his side if she let him.

"Afternoon Hannah," he said as she reached him.

"Mason, what brings you here?"

He smiled and took his hat off, "I wanted to come see you."

She smiled and tucked a lose strand of hair behind her ear, "Is that so?"

Even Hannah looked different now, it was as if this cloud of fog that kept skewed his outlook on life had been lifted, "Yes indeed, would you like to go for a walk with me?"

He saw her hesitate slightly but then she nodded, "Of course, I could use some fresh air before I have to go to the sisters meeting."

They walked in silence for a short while and as if they were both searching for words they spoke at the exact same time, "I wanted...." Mason started.

"What did you..." Hannah interrupted and then giggled.

"Well, it spent some time thinking about what you said."

Bending down he picked a small yellow flower and then handed it to her, "I have decided to stay here in Lancaster. My father was willing to baptize me so I'm once again part of the community."

The look on her face was priceless, and the way her eyes lit up made him want to kiss her there and then, but he refused to ruin a perfect moment.

"You did?" she asked breathlessly.

"Yes, you see, I left here thinking that the world was what I needed, and for some time it was fun, but after I returned here and saw you again, I realized what a big mistake that was."

He could tell she didn't know what to say by the way her mouth fell opened and closed, so he continued, "Hannah, I know a lot has happened and you're afraid of commitment, but I've always loved you and I want to spend the rest of my life proving that to you."

"Mason..." she started and looked down at the flower in her hand, "what if you decide to leave again?"

"I won't, my life is here now, my family and friends, and I want to be where you are." He stepped closer and cupped the side of her face, "Only if that is what you want."

Hannah leaned into his touch and a single tear ran down the side of her cheek which he wiped with the pad of his thumb.

"Do you promise to stay?" she asked in a trembling voice.

"I promise."

"Good because my heart would never survive if you broke it a second time," she said and walked into his arms.

"I'll protect it with my life."

****

Four months later, Hannah and Mason finally got married. Mason had laid down his former life and found his own feet amongst his fellow Amish folk, but he would never have been able to do this without Hannah. She was his beacon in his dark night.

BONUS STORY
PART ONE

She felt a mix of relief and despair as she watched the Boston skyline fade away. She felt a mix of relief and despair. She knew she would never come back to her beloved hometown. There was nothing left for her there. In fact, all she had left fit into a small carry-on bag. Her life had shattered, and most of the pieces had blown away in the wind.

She grabbed her phone and read Colt's email again.

I am a simple man. I own the Lone Moon Ranch in Helena, Montana. I've lived here all my life. I am 26 now. I am looking for a wife, someone who can take over the household duties; cooking, cleaning and such. Also, to assist with various chores around the ranch. I need someone who is not deterred by early mornings and not afraid of hard work. In return, I will make sure you are well-taken care of. I am seeking a partner, not a companion. Please contact me if you have questions.

He didn't include a photo and she never asked for one. It didn't matter what he looked like. She appreciated the fact that he sounded very businesslike in his email. That's what this was – a business deal. She had placed an ad on a mail order bride site - not for love, but for security. Colt fit the bill. He needed a wife and she needed an escape. Of course, he had no clue what she was escaping from. She hadn't been completely honest with him about her past.

She tossed her phone back into her purse. She rubbed her thumb against her ring finger as she laid back against her seat and closed her eyes. She didn't want to think about Nick. But he was always there, lurking just below the surface. She could picture his dark eyes and dangerous smile. When they met, he made her feel alive and invincible. Loving Nick was like grabbing hold of a lightning bolt. He had lit her up and then burned her to ashes.

They got married a month after their first date. Nick was wild and impulsive that way, and she couldn't deny him anything. But Nick was also a drunk and a gambler. He got so wasted on their wedding night that he passed out in the hotel lobby. Three months in, he had blown through all her savings. He became violent and erratic when the money ran out. He isolated her from her family and her friends so she had no one to help her. And she couldn't leave him. They were each other's obsession even though he scared her. But then one night he crashed into another car and almost killed the driver. She could picture his face the day of sentencing. Six years. And the way he looked at her the last time she went to visit him, to tell him she had filed for divorce. She lied to him and told him it was all his fault. But she couldn't lie to herself. She knew she was just as much to blame. Maybe he struck the match but they had both danced within the flames.

Their 2-year marriage had stripped her of everything. She lost her condo, her car, and even her job. Her parents had both passed way, and both her brother and sister had given up on her. She needed to start over. And there were worst ways to do that than a beautiful ranch in Montana. So, she bought a plane ticket and a new dress using the only credit card she had left and swore to do her very best to not look back.

***

Colt Malone stood inside Helena Regional Airport. He jiggled his truck keys impatiently against his thigh. Joelle's flight had been delayed. And while he was many things, patient was not one of them. It was a trait that had never come easily to him. Mainly because he rarely liked to be idle.

Nearly every woman that walked past him, smiled. Women had always noticed him. But it had been a long time since one had shared his life or his bed. Not since Ashlyn. They had grown up together. He chased her from the moment he was big enough to run. He couldn't recall a moment of his life that he didn't love her. She had been his best friend and then his lover. But Ashlyn wanted to chase something of her own. Her dreams had taken her far from Montana and far from him. She was in California now. He used to think they'd get married and build a life together. He used to think love matter more than anything. Now he knew better. Love broke you in ways that would never heal. And he didn't intend to ever give someone that kind of power over him again.

He made the ranch his whole life. His father had died three years prior, and he had no other family. When his father died, the ranch and all the responsibility of it became his. It was a huge undertaking. The ranch was financially in bad shape. It was burden his father had never shared with him, but something he inherited just the same.

Things still weren't great. He worked from sun up to sun down, but the ranch was still in jeopardy. He had to lay off most of the staff. He had taken out new loans to pay off old ones. But the ranch was still in debt. He knew he didn't have time to be angry but he was. He was angry that his father hadn't been a better businessman. He was angry at his mother for leaving when he was young. He was angry at the hand life and love had dealt him.

He couldn't say what came over him the night he went online and found the mail order bride website. He guessed it was his loneliness. He wanted to come home to a hot meal and a warm body. He didn't want someone to fall in love with but he did want a partner. Someone to share his burdens and his life. Joelle's ad had stood out to him. She was beautiful but haunted. Long, dark hair and big expressive eyes. She looked like a painting from another time and place. She seemed like a woman that could possess a man and make him beg at her feet, and yet gave him the sense that she didn't want to possess anyone. What she wanted was security. A place in the world that belonged to her. He could give her that, even if he could never give her his heart.

The gate opened, and a rush of people came toward him. Cole scanned the crowd looking for her. He had looked at her picture a dozen times. He had stared into her hazel eyes and memorized the color of her lips and the curve of her neck. His finger had traced each wave of her long, raven hair. But that picture had in no way prepared him for the real-life version.

He called her name and she walked toward him, her cheeks flush and her hair slightly tangled. She was smiling, but it didn't quite reach her eyes.

"Colt?"

"Hello," he said. His voice came out slightly gruff.

"Hi." She hesitated for a moment, but then sat down her bag and leaned into him.

He didn't think, he just put his arms around her and closed his eyes. He felt his whole body respond to hers, full and warm against him. She smelled of a lavender and citrus. And when she pulled back to look up at him, he felt breathless for the first time in a long time. Yep, she could awaken a hunger in a man and he was in no way immune; and it was a hunger he had almost forgotten was there. His pulse quickened, and this animal desire to ravage her was stirring inside. He swallowed, and took a long, shaky breath.

"I'm glad I'm here," she said softly.

"So am I."

They stood for a moment, still half in each other's arm. He took another breath and steadied himself.

"We should get going Do you have more bags?" he asked.

She smiled again in a sad sort of way. He saw something in her eyes for the briefest of moments, but then it was gone.

"This is all I have." She gestured toward the bag at her feet. "I meant it when I said I was looking forward to a fresh start."

He picked up the bag for her. "My trucks just outside then," he said. "We have an appointment at the courthouse in less than an hour."

She nodded. They had done the paperwork online, and obtain their marriage license. He had told her he didn't see any reason to put things off, and so he made an appointment at the courthouse for them to be married that afternoon. She didn't seem to want to wait either.

They exited the airport and Joelle's breath hitched as she took in the landscape. The blue sky was cloudless and seemed to have no end.

The land before them was flat and rugged until your eyes found the mountains jutting into the heavens.

"It's so beautiful," she said softly.

"It is," he agreed. He had never strayed far from home. The soul of him came from the land and those mountains.

They reached his pickup truck, and he tossed her bag into the bed of it. The truck was painted a fire engine red and it was well loved and taken care of.

"After you." He opened the passenger side door, and then without thinking he reached down and touched her cheek. This made her lips part slightly.

An invitation?

Her lips were as red as his truck and he couldn't seem to look away. Slowly he bent down, letting his own lips graze her's. His hands fell to her waist, and he pulled her body to his. He kissed her, tasting the sweetness of her. She didn't respond to him at first. But he felt the exact moment when she let go. She molded herself to him, and her body hummed. She made a sexy, breathy sound and it about did him in. Somehow he knew she had the same kind of demons that he did. She buried things too. Maybe like him, she still held out hope that one day she'd find redemption.

She pulled away first. She stared at him, her breath ragged.

"Colt, I didn't come here to fall for you."

Trying to regain his composure he said, "I didn't bring you here to fall in love."

"Before we do this, I need you to promise me again. Love is not part of the agreement."

"I do. And I'll keep my promise." He nodded toward the open truck door and ran his fingers through his hair. She was holding his gaze, searching.

"So will I," she said and got up into the truck. They were on the road a moment later, heading for the courthouse on the other side of town.

***

Joelle tried to stop her hands from shaking. She and Colt had arrived at the courthouse, and she could hear the Judge and Colt talking. But all she could think of was that moment she spotted him in the airport. He had on a pair of Wrangler's that fit him well and a button-down shirt. Cowboy boots of course and she had spotted a matching cowboy hat in the truck. He was also sporting a five o'clock shadow even though it was only noon. He wore it well. Too well. He was quite possibly the most handsome man she had even laid eyes on. His auburn hair that curled at the ends and those smoky eyes rimmed with lashes that went on for days. And when he kissed her...

"We're ready." Colt touched her arm lightly. The Judge was just beside him.

"But are you ready my dear?" he asked. He had a soft voice and a kindly face.

"I do – I mean I am," she stammered. They both smiled at her and she laughed nervously. Colt had her undone and that was not part of the plan.

The simple ceremony took less than ten minutes. When it concluded, Colt leaned in and kissed her again. This kiss was softer and sweeter. It held a promise instead of passion. It told her he would be there and he would take care of her.

"Let's go home," he said.

It was a good twenty minutes before they reached the ranch. Colt turned down a rocky drive. Lone Moon Ranch sat a mile off the main road with rolling hills on either side. The main house was average in size, painted red with a white a trim. A barn sat directly to the left of the house, and acres of pasture and field to the right. She breathed in the smell of cut grass and watched as hundreds of dandelions danced in the late afternoon breeze. She spotted several cows in the pasture, and could make out the sound of horses nearby.

He put the car in park right in front of the house. He got out and came around to open the door for her. They stood in the driveway for a long time in silence. He was letting her take everything in. She had never seen so much land and beauty in all her life. She felt like she had been dropped in the middle of nowhere, and the middle of nowhere looked a lot like paradise.

"Hello!" A middle-aged woman came down the front porch steps. She was drying her hands on the apron she wore. Her graying hair was pulled back into a tight bun, and she had a big smile on her face. She came toward Joelle, and pulled her into a tight hug.

"My goodness, you are gorgeous." She pulled back, holding Joelle at arm's length. Then she leaned in and hugged her again. "We are so happy to have you. And congratulations to you both!" She turned to him then, and he bent so she could kiss his cheek. She looked at him with such affection that it made Joelle smile.

"This is Minnie," Colt said. "Minnie, this is Joelle."

"You can call me Jo."

Minnie turned back and hugged her again.

"Minnie is a dear friend," he explained. "She comes by once or twice a week to help tidy up or cook one of her delicious meals. I don't deserve her at all, but I honestly don't know what I would do without her."

"Oh shush." She slapped him playfully on the arm. "I love you like my own son. And how I wish I could do more for you, love." Her eyes got misty. "But here you are now." She turned back to Joelle. "I am just so happy that Colt has found someone to love again."

Colt cleared his throat uncomfortably and she got the impression that Minnie had no idea how they had met. And maybe she would be a bit taken aback if she knew he had basically gone online and ordered up a bride.

"Well, I am happy to be here. So happy," Joelle said. "Colt has just stolen my heart and I don't ever want it back."

Minnie clapped her hands in delight, smiling brightly at them. He was giving her a look, and she gave him a sideways smile.

"Well, come on in. You must be tired and famished. I have dinner all ready." She directed them inside, like a shepherd herding her flock.

Once inside the house, she took a moment to look around her new home. All the rooms were big and open, with high ceilings and lots of windows. The living room was to her left, and a large stone fireplace stood against the back wall. He didn't have a whole lot of furniture, a leather couch, and two big chairs.

She made her way to the kitchen, which was also airy and full of lots of natural light. A large island sat in the center and a small breakfast nook in the corner. The dining room sat off to the right, and both rooms blended well together.

"There's a roast warming in the oven. And biscuits on the table," Minnie said. "You've outdone yourself again," he told her.

"Oh, don't fuss on me. You sit down and enjoy your dinner. I'll be around tomorrow, Jo, to help you settle in."

"Thank you – so much," she said.

Minnie smiled and touched her cheek. "You're going to be very happy here," she promised and then she was gone.

He glanced toward the dining room table. "Shall we?" he asked.

She nodded, her stomach rumbling at the thought. She hadn't eaten breakfast or lunch that day. In fact, she hadn't eaten much at all lately. Certainly, nothing that resembled a home cooked meal.

They ate in silence for several minutes. She savored the biscuits dipped in honey. She glanced up at him, the late afternoon sun poured in through a window, and she could see the flecks of red in his hair.

"I'm sorry you didn't have any family or friends here today," he said.

"I don't have a family. None that speak to me anyway. And no real friends either," she told him. "It's just me."

"Why doesn't your family speak to you?" he asked.

She looked up, meeting his gaze. "My parents died last year. It was a car accident. That sent my spiraling a bit. I didn't always make the best decisions. My brother and sister are both older than me. I guess they handle things better than I do. She has two kids and he owns his own business. I'm the black sheep and they finally threw in the towel."

"Doesn't seem fair," he said. "You're family. They shouldn't just turn their backs on you."

"I don't blame them," she replied honestly. "I hurt them a lot. They felt like they needed to protect themselves."

He sat back in his chair, holding her gaze across the table. "Is that why you left? Why you married me?"

"I don't have anything, Colt. I'm embarrassed to say that, but it's the truth. But now I'm your wife. And here we are together, and I want this to work. I want this ranch to be as much mine as it is yours. I want us to take care of it together."

"And you mean that?"

"I do."

"You know, it's just me, too. Sure – I have friends. Wonderful friends. But no family. This ranch is all I have, and I work every day to hold on to it for me... For us." He paused still watching her. "And I'm sorry about your parents. I never knew my mother, but my daddy passed away three years ago. So, I mean it – I am sorry."

"It's been over a year. You would think it would hurt a little less by now."

"It won't ever hurt any less. You just learn to live with it."

They took their time finishing dinner. She liked talking to him and he seemed to like to listen. She talked a lot about Boston. It was her first love after all. They also talked about the ranch, and she asked him questions about his life growing up.

When they finished, he stood and pushed his chair back heavily. "I get up at five. We should go to bed."

Bed?

His eyes had turned to smolder. Slowly, she stood as well.

"Okay."

"Jo, listen - I've never had a woman in my bed who didn't want to be there," he began. "But it's been a long time. So, I am hoping you will join me in it tonight." With that, he stepped around the table and walked past her. She listened to the echo of his boots as he went upstairs.

She felt rooted in place for several seconds, twisting her dinner napkin back and forth in her hands. The attraction she felt toward him was undeniable. And even hours later, she could still remember the taste of his lips on hers. A slight tremor went through her at the memory. It had been a long time for her as well. And he was her husband...

He was sitting on the bed in the first bedroom. There was a large bay window to the left with a window seat. The setting sun painted the room a dusty rose color.

"I don't sleep in the master bedroom," he explained. He watched her as she scanned the bedroom, taking it all in.

"Why?" she asked softly.

"It's not mine. Never was, and I don't see how it could ever be. Is that a problem?"

She shook her head no. She was still standing in the doorway, and they watched each other across the room. She could see his chest rise and fall with each breath. He seemed to be tracing her whole body with his eyes.

"Come to bed," he told her. His voice was a husky whisper.

Again, a tremor went through her. She felt an ache and longing deep inside. She had not just been alone; she had been lonely. And she had been that way long before Nick got arrested.

"Colt." She came to him, straddling his waist and pushing him down on the bed. She leaned over, creating a canopy with her hair. It blocked out the world, so all that was left was the two of them. They held on to each other. Some moments thrashing against the night and all the loneliness that had held them captive. They were iron and lace, colliding in moments of raw, insatiable need. And in other moments, they were soft and gentle and warm like a summer breeze. Their bodies lifting and swaying like waves to the shore.

PART TWO

Joelle rolled over in bed, pulling the covers around her. She opened her eyes to see that the sun was making its way across the sky. She sighed happily. Her whole body felt sated and relaxed. She smiled, thinking of the night before. She could feel her insides vibrate and stir. She wasn't sure any man had ever made her feel that way. She was literally humming from the inside out. She was more than satisfied, yet the hunger for him lingered.

"Jo."

She jumped slightly, then turned back over in bed. Colt was standing over her, completely dressed. He was clean shaven and he smelled wonderful. She reached out, her hand caressing his.

"Come back to bed," she told him.

"Back to bed?" he repeated. "You need to get up."

She blinked and sat up. She wasn't dressed, so she pulled the sheet up around her.

"What's wrong?"

"There's no breakfast made. And I am heading out. There is housework to be done. I thought we discussed all this."

"Colt..."

"I need a partner, Jo."

"I know that." She blinked several more times, pushing back tears that suddenly burned her eyes. "We were partners last night," she said softly.

"I have to start my day. I'll eat some biscuits left over from last night. But I'll be back at noon, and I'd like something hot waiting for me." He turned then and stalked out of the bedroom.

She smacks away a few tears that had managed to escape. She got out of bed, pulling the sheet along with her. She needed a shower and she needed coffee. And she needed to get herself in check. She couldn't lay in bed daydreaming about him all day. He was a business decision, nothing more.

She padded down the hall, the floor cold against her bare feet. Her clothes were still in her suitcase which she'd left in the foyer. The house was silent as she made her way carefully down the winding staircase. Just as she reached the landing, the front door swung open.

A man stood there looking like John Wayne come back to life. He was most likely in his forties. But a life working under the sun had leathered his skin, and it made him appear older.

"Well, I beg your pardon," he said. He respectfully glanced away as she clutched the sheet tighter.

"Who are you?" she asked.

"Jeff Loggings, darling," he said. "You must be Joelle."

"Good morning." Minnie came through the door but stopped in her tracks when she saw Joelle. "Goodness, Jeff." She slapped his arm. "We're sorry to barge in, honey. Go on up and get yourself ready. It looks like you had a wonderful wedding night." She gave Joelle a wink, and then pushed Jeff toward the kitchen.

She grabbed her suitcase and ran back up the stairs. She was out of the shower and dressed in ten minutes. As she headed back downstairs, the smell of perked coffee wafting up to her.

"I hope you don't mind, I got things started," Jeff said, nodding toward the coffee pot.

"Not at all. Thank you." He handed her a steaming cup. Minnie was bustling around, going back and forth between the refrigerator and the pantry.

"How are you settling in?" Jeff asked as they sat down at the table.

"Just fine."

"Is that so?" Jeff gave her a look that remaindered her of her father.

"I slept in," she admitted. She glanced at the clock hanging on the wall. It was a quarter after seven.

"Getting up at dawn takes getting used to. You'll get into the swing of it. Minnie, Colt and I have been doing it our whole lives. I wouldn't know how to sleep in even if I could."

"I could teach you," she said with a smile.

He returned it. "Don't let him scare you off," he said a moment later.

"Scare me off?"

"Colt is certainly rough around the edges. But beneath all that there is a heart of gold. He's just been lonely too long. And he feels the weight of the world on his shoulders. When his daddy died, it about did him in. That was all the family he had, and he was just here one day and gone the next. I don't think Colt even realizes how much it affected him. How much it broke his heart."

She took a long sip from her cup. She certainly knew about heartbreak.

"He doesn't scare me a bit," she said. "I'm quite fond of him." She was surprised to hear some truth in her words.

Jeff leaned across the table and said quietly, "I know how you met. Minnie doesn't. God don't tell her! But I know. And I know Colt told you he wasn't looking for love."

"He did. I'm not looking for love either," she confessed.

"Is that so? Now, darling, everyone is looking for love. Surely, you know that."

"I've had love."

"And how did that work out?"

"Lousy," she replied. "So lousy that it turned me off to the prospect altogether."

Jeff laughed. He had a genuine twinkle in his eye. "If I had a nickel for every time someone said those words. For every time I said those words."

"But aren't you and Minnie married?" she asked.

"Yes. Third time for me, though. I was pretty bitter on love, but there it was all these years – right in front of my face." He stood up then, draining the last of his coffee.

"Minnie, I am heading out," he called. She was just coming out of the pantry. She came over and kissed his cheek. "It was nice meeting you, Jo."

"It was very nice to meet you, too," she told him.

"I'll see you soon." He put on his hat and tipped it toward her. Then he headed out the back door.

***

Minnie stayed for a few hours. She started a pot of chili, and she showed her around the house. It was almost noon when she left, promising to be back the next day. Joelle started a load of laundry and put some cornbread in the oven. It was ready twenty minutes later when Colt came in.

"Smells good," he said.

"Wash up," she told him.

She gave her a tired smile, and memories of the night before flooded her again. She felt her cheeks go warm and her body go flush as he brushed past her. He stood at the kitchen sink for several minutes, washing away the morning. When he finally sat back down, she placed a hot bowl of chili in front of him.

"I have to go into town this afternoon," he said. He turned to his chili and downed half the bowl in a matter of seconds.

"Should I come?" she asked.

"No need. I have an appointment at the bank. I'm a little behind on the mortgage."

She looked up at him. "What do you mean?"

"My daddy was a great man, but his finances were a mess when he died. I've been working day and night to get things in order again. But times are hard."

She dropped her spoon into her bowl. Bits of chili splashed across the table. "I don't understand. I thought you owned this ranch."

"The bank owns the ranch, Jo."

"But you said you could take care of a wife." She didn't know why she suddenly felt so panicky, but she did.

"I can. The manager is a buddy of mine. Everything will be alright," he said. "I'm doing my best. I've been running uphill for three years now."

"I don't know what to say." And she didn't.

"Listen, I apologize if what I said made you believe I owned this ranch right out. I don't. But I hope to someday. I can tell you this, I will always take care of you. But this isn't a prison, it's a marriage. You can leave anytime you want if this isn't what you want."

"Do you want me to leave?"

"No – I don't."

"I just – I can't go back." Tears burned her eyes. She couldn't look up at him. But she heard him push his chair back and come around the table.

"Then don't." He reached down and tilted her head back so she was looking at him. Then he bent and kissed her lips, softly at first and then harder. He pulled her up from the chair and against him. She wanted him. Wanted him right then and there.

As if reading her mind, he lifted her up and onto the table. He came down on top of her, the weight of him making her whole body ache with want. She arched into him and he moaned softly, his breath warm against her ear. And when he took her, she clung to him as if she was lost at sea and he was the only thing keeping her from drowning completely.

***

Colt left the bank feeling uneasy. He was almost three months behind on the mortgage. Not to mention the taxes were due. He had one month to catch up on payments or the ranch will be put up for auction. He hadn't a clue how he would manage, but he was certainly going to try. He just had to work harder. He knew how to do that.

He spent the next few weeks doing just that and showing Joelle the ins and outs of ranch life. She was able to help with some of the manual labor, but not much. He was simply stronger and had been doing it his whole life. There was always hay to cut, bale and stack. Always a fence that needed mending or manure to haul. Joelle helped with other things. She worked a lot in the garden and with the animals. She seemed to enjoy the animals more than anything, especially the horses. He liked watching her with them. In fact, over the next few days, he caught himself watching her more and more.

He also liked coming home to her – most days. It had become painfully obvious she had never kept house before. She could cook - sure, but nothing from scratch. And she tried baking but burned practically everything. She told him that she cleaned every day. He was sure she did. But it was more like tidying up here and there. She had yet to give the whole ranch the good scrubbing that it needed. It was gnawing at him. They had fought about it more than once.

"I just don't know what you want from me!" she told him.

"You know exactly what I want, Jo. Come on."

"A housemaid."

"A partner! Don't act like I don't work myself into an early grave. Is it so much to ask to have a clean house and a decent dinner?"

She stormed out of the room. He found her an hour later, listening to music in the living room. It was a slow song, something country and twangy. The sun had gone down, and the living room was in shadows. He held out his hand to her, and she took it. They swayed together to the music.

"I am trying," she said sadly.

"I know." He held her, getting lost in the moment.

They went upstairs a little later. This is what he longed for all day. It didn't matter if they had bickered all day, he couldn't wait to get under the blankets with her each night. She was beautiful and soft. She awakened things in him that had been dormant for too long. In those moments, he could care less if she knew how to bake bread or use a vacuum. He was completely under her spell.

***

Joelle sat drinking her third cup of coffee. It was late in the day. Colt would be home soon. A part of her hummed with the anticipation of seeing him. The other part of her worried. She glanced around the kitchen and dining room, searching for some spot she hadn't dusted or dish she hadn't washed. She knew he was disappointed. She was not a housewife. At least not one that lived up to his standards. But she was trying. She was becoming more and more aware of how hard she was trying. How much she wanted to make him happy. That made her nervous. There were days when all she thought about was the moment he would walk through the door.

"Hey," he came in just then. He looked rugged and handsome, tired from a long day. "Something smells sweet."

"I baked a cheesecake today," she said proudly. "And I didn't burn it."

"I didn't know you had to actually bake a cheesecake."

"Exactly," she replied. They both smiled.

He sat down, mail in his hand. He began to shuffle through it as she got up to make him a sandwich.

"Jo, why would a lawyer be writing to you?" he questioned.

She stopped mid-step and turned back toward him. "What?"

He held up one of the envelopes and gave her a questioning stare. "Well?"

"I don't know," she said. "Let me have it." She snatched it from her hand.

"What's going on?" he asked with a frown.

"I think it's just about some property I use to own," she lied.

He stood up and came toward her. "Then let's open it." His voice had gone cold.

"It's personal."

"You're my wife..."

"Colt, please."

"Is this about us, Joelle? What are you trying to do – what are you after?"

"After?" she repeated. "What does that mean?"

"Just open the envelope!"

"You think I trying to take something from you? After the past four weeks, that's what you think of me?"

"I don't know what to think. Just open it."

She threw the letter at him, hot tears springing up in her eyes. "This has nothing to do with you. It's about me. I was married before, Colt. He was a drunk and an abuser, and he's in prison now. And now you know."

He took a step back as if he'd been punched in the gut. "You were married before?"

"I was. He took everything I had. He gambled it away. He drank it away. He became violet when it all ran out. And he almost killed someone." Tears were streaming down her cheeks now. "I'm sorry I didn't tell you. I should have."

"Then, why didn't you?"

"A lot of reasons. Mostly because I didn't want you to know. I didn't think you'd want me if you knew, and I needed you to want me. And I was embarrassed. I had been such a fool for him. And it's hard to admit our mistakes sometimes..."

"You lied to me."

"I'm sorry."

"So am I." He turned and walked out the back door.

"Colt," she said. The tears were raging now. She sunk down on the kitchen tile and cried her eyes out.

PART THREE

Colt didn't sleep at all that night. He stayed downstairs on the couch. He could hear Jo above him, pacing the floor. He could hear when she cried. He wanted to go to her, but he couldn't. Finally, he got up and got in the shower. Joelle had finally fallen asleep, and he didn't wake her before he left. He drove into town. Ashlyn was coming to meet him.

He sat at a back table of the local diner. He and Ashlyn had come here almost every weekend when they were dating. He thought about how young and free they had been. He was still young, but he didn't feel very free anymore.

"Colt."

He looked up, and there she was. She looked just the same, if not more beautiful. He stood up as she fluttered into his arms. When they sat down, she reached across the table and held his hand.

"I've missed you," she said. "I heard you got married."

"I did," he replied with a sad smile.

"I'm happy for you. I mean that," she told him.

He nodded slowly. "I know you do."

"Do you love her?" she asked.

Did he?

He knew he had been falling for her more every day. It hadn't been his plan. But it had happened just the same.

"Love is hard," he said.

"It's not," she replied. "Not everyone runs from love, Colt. Not everyone is as big a fool as I am." She squeezed his hand and then let it go. She shuffled around in her purse and then pulled out an envelope. She slid it across the table.

"This should take care of things," she told him.

"I'll pay you back, I swear."

"I know," she said softly. "I am just glad I could help. I love that ranch. And your daddy would be real proud of you."

"Would he?"

"Believe me, he would. You've built a nice life for yourself. You should let yourself enjoy it."

He smiled at her across the table. "Maybe you're right. It meant a lot to see you, but I should go." He stood up, sliding the envelope into his pocket. He came to the table, bent down and kissed the top of her head. "Thank you."

She nodded, reaching up and taking his hand one more time. She held it for a moment and then let him go for good.

***

Colt had been gone all day. It was getting late, and Joelle was drained. She had packed a bag, and she planned on leaving in the morning. Her heart restricted at the thought. Despite her best efforts, she was falling for him. But the truth was out now, and he didn't want her anymore.

"Hi." Colt appeared in the doorway. "I want you to take a ride with me."

She didn't question him. She just got up and followed him outside. It was cold, and she shivered slightly. The world was dark, not even the moon was out as they headed for the barn. One of the horses was out, already saddled.

They rode for a long time without speaking. She felt like they were the only people left in the world. And when they reached a meadow, he got down off the horse and brought her with him. They sunk down in the cool grass, under the sable sky and made love. It was slow and sweet and tender. So much so that she felt like her heart might burst.

"Every day for the past month I have asked myself the same two questions," he said, lying beside her.

"And what are they?" she asked.

"What am I doing? What are we doing?"

"Come up with any answers?"

He gave her a sideways smile. "Some. But they terrify me."

"Why?"

"Because I'm falling in love with you. I broke my promise. And you lied."

"I'm sorry."

"I know. And I know why you did it. You deserve better than him. And I'm sorry for what he did to you." He reached over and took her hand.

"I didn't want to fall for you either. But I did. A little more every day. Colt – please understand. I didn't know how kind a man could be. And yes, you want things your way. Your stubborn and a perfectionist. And you work too hard. But you're also loving and compassionate. Strong and supportive." She turned to face him.

"Jo..."

"I fell for you, too." She had come here to escape love. But everything catches up to you eventually. No point is running. And she supposed she always knew deep down it would be a losing battle. The first time she saw him, she knew. The first time he kissed her, she knew. And when they made love...well, she certainly knew then.

"I promise never to keep anything from you again," she said.

"And I promise to take care of you every day of my life."

"And I promise to love you, Colt. And never leave you."

"I promise to love you and worship you." He kissed her softly. "This time, I'll keep my promises."

She smiled against his lips. "So will I."

THE END